S0-CSZ-184

For my beloved nephew Huzaifah Bangali,
your presence makes every celebration an exciting one – Z.T.

For my Dado – A.T.

Text copyright © 2022 by Zeba Talkhani
Illustrations copyright © 2022 by Abeeha Tariq

First published in 2022 by Scholastic Children's Books, a division of Scholastic Ltd.
Scholastic UK Ltd., No 1 London Bridge, London SE1 9BG

All rights reserved. Published by Scholastic Press, an imprint of Scholastic Inc.,
Publishers since 1920. SCHOLASTIC, SCHOLASTIC PRESS, and associated logos
are trademarks and/or registered trademarks of Scholastic Inc.

The publisher does not have any control over and does not assume any
responsibility for author or third-party websites or their content.

No part of this publication may be reproduced, stored in a retrieval system,
or transmitted in any form or by any means, electronic, mechanical,
photocopying, recording, or otherwise, without written permission of the publisher.
For information regarding permission, write to Scholastic Inc., Attention:
Permissions Department, 557 Broadway, New York, NY 10012.

This book is a work of fiction. Names, characters, places, and incidents
are either the product of the author's imagination or are used fictitiously,
and any resemblance to actual persons, living or dead, business establishments,
events, or locales is entirely coincidental.

Library of Congress Cataloging-in-Publication Data available

ISBN 978-1-338-87781-6

10 9 8 7 6 5 4 3 2 1   24 25 26 27 28

Printed in the U.S.A. 76
This edition first printing, February 2024

THE MOST EXCITING EID

ZEBA TALKHANI

ABEEHA TARIQ

Scholastic Press • New York

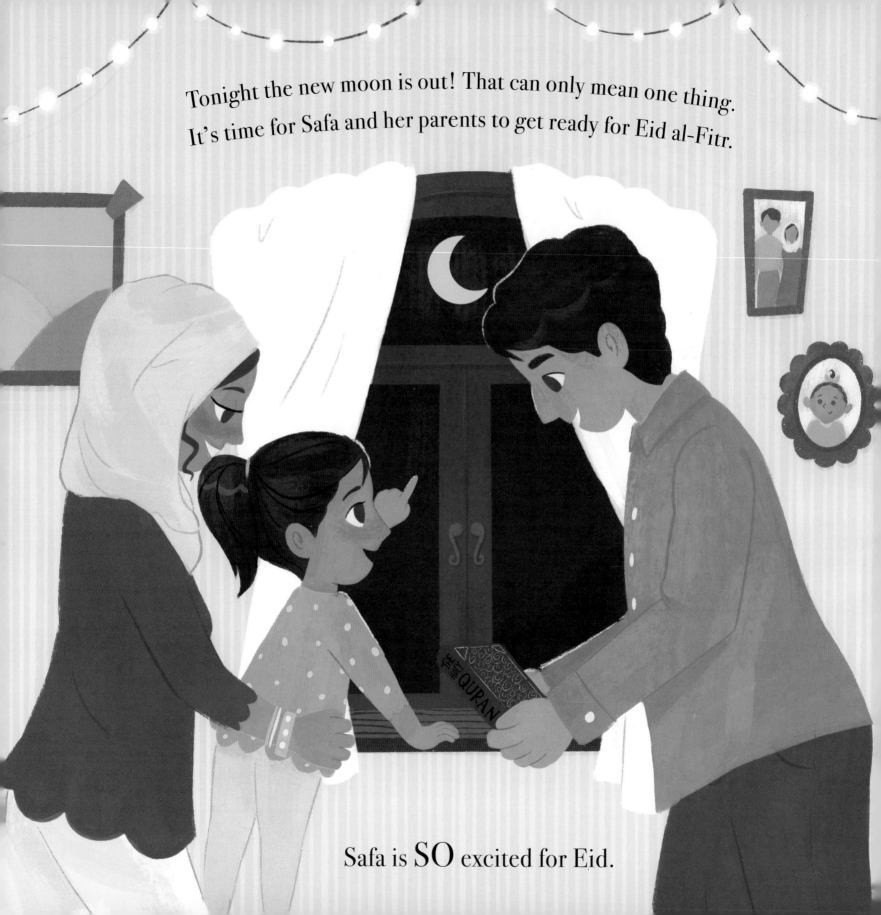

Tonight the new moon is out! That can only mean one thing.
It's time for Safa and her parents to get ready for Eid al-Fitr.

Safa is SO excited for Eid.

Mom draws pretty **henna** patterns on their hands, like every year.

Dad brings down a box of Eid decorations from the attic.
Safa SQUEALS at the sight of them and helps.

"Time for bed, Safa," says Dad when they're done.

But Safa is just too EXCITED to fall asleep!

She thinks of everything she is
looking forward to tomorrow:

yummy food . . .

EID

gifts . . .

brand-new clothes . . .

and the big family gathering!

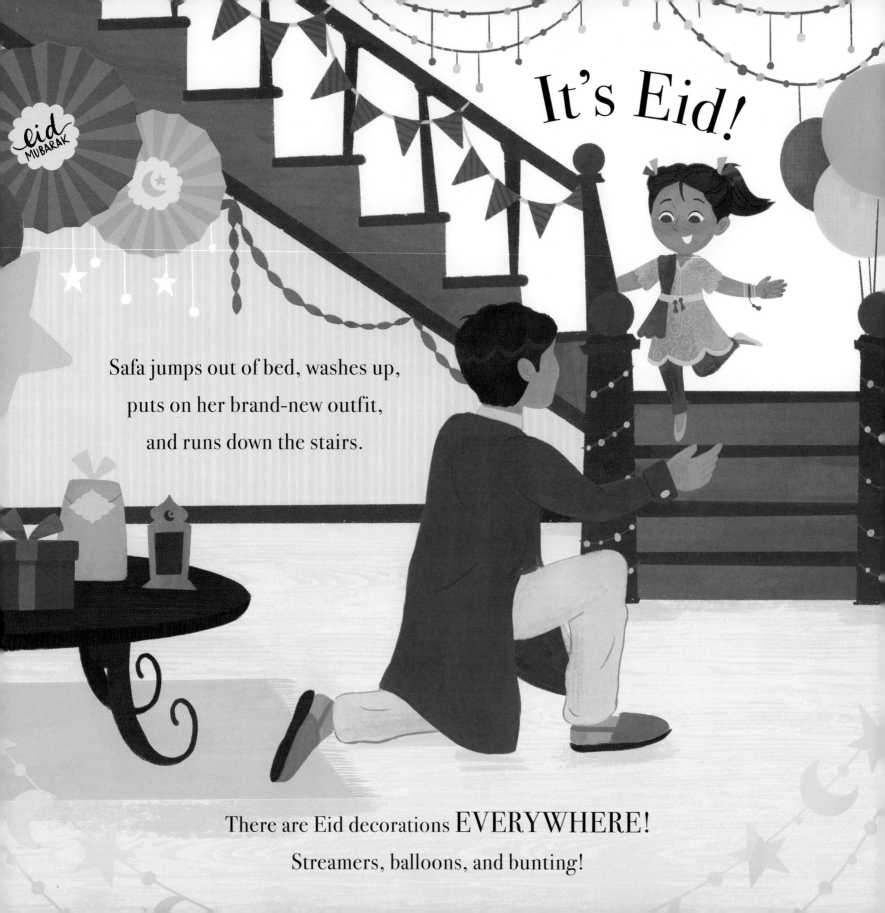

It's Eid!

Safa jumps out of bed, washes up,
puts on her brand-new outfit,
and runs down the stairs.

There are Eid decorations EVERYWHERE!
Streamers, balloons, and bunting!

Eid
MUBARAK

When it's time to pray, Safa asks Allah for a new doll, a colored pencil set, and a bicycle.

"Eid Mubarak!"

Now the guests are arriving, too!
Even Alissa, her cousin, has come over.

"As-salamu alaykum!
Eid Mubarak!"

"Wa alaykumu s-salam, Safa!
Eid Mubarak!"

"Let's open our presents."
Safa gets EVERYTHING she
asked for . . . even a shiny bicycle
with a big pink bow on it.

She gets on her bike and starts
riding it. Alissa shouts after her,
but Safa doesn't feel like sharing.
She has wanted this bike

FOREVER!

"Safa!"

Mom calls Safa into the kitchen.
"Let's do something special together,
now that you're old enough!"

Safa loves doing special things with Mom.
Mom hands Safa two huge bags.

"Eid is about sharing our joys and our food with those who might be in need," says Mom with a big smile.

Safa remembers she didn't share her bike with Alissa.

"Hurry, Safa!"

Then she puts some of the treats she received into the bags Mom packed.

When Mom knocks on a neighbor's door, a lady with tired eyes opens the door.

"Eid Mubarak! This is for you!"

The lady smiles and no longer looks tired.

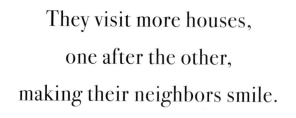

They visit more houses, one after the other, making their neighbors smile.

Safa is beaming, seeing her neighbors smile is making her happier than opening presents. Maybe sharing isn't that bad.

There was just one bag left. "Where are we going now?"

"It's a surprise!"

Grandma opens the door with the brightest smile.

Grandpa scoops Safa into a big hug.

Safa is **very excited** to share biryani, kebabs, and samosas with them.

On her way home, Safa realizes she felt happy after
sharing her treats with all her neighbors . . .

And now she **can't wait** to share her gifts and play together with Alissa.

"Where did you go?
I was looking for you everywhere."

"I'm sorry, Alissa. Next year, let's do this all together!"
After all, what makes Eid exciting is
sharing special moments with the people we love.

Glossary

Allah means "God" in Arabic, and Muslims around the world refer to their God as Allah.

"Allah Hafiz" means "May God protect you" and is a common way among Muslims to say goodbye.

"As-salamu alaykum" is a greeting that means "Peace be upon you."

Eid al-Fitr is celebrated by Muslims around the world. It is a time to come together with family and friends and for taking care of the people around us. In Arabic, Eid al-Fitr means "Festival of Breaking Fast." Eid al-Fitr marks the end of Ramadan.

"Eid Mubarak!" is the most common way to wish each other a Happy Eid. Mubarak means "blessed," and Muslims wish each other a blessed Eid.

Ramadan is when Muslims fast all day for a month. Fasting means you can't eat or drink anything! The end of Ramadan depends on when the new moon is spotted.

Sawm means "fasting" and it's one of the five pillars of Islam. It's important for all healthy adult Muslims to fast from dawn to dusk during the month of Ramadan. Fasting helps Muslims feel gratitude for the blessings they might take for granted, such as endless food and clean water. Fasting allows Muslims to understand those in need.

"Wa alaykumu s-salam" is the response to "As-salamu alaykum" and it means the same.

We celebrate Eid al-Fitr in different ways around the world, but it always starts with a special morning prayer. On Eid we also always see our loved ones and enjoy traditional Eid food.

Zakat is another pillar of Islam. It encourages all Muslims to give a portion of their earnings to charity. It's an important part of Eid. Zakat can take the form of money, gifts, or food.